The Village of a Hundred Smiles

and other stories

Text by Barrie Baker
Art by Stéphane Jorisch

Annick Press Ltd.
Toronto/New York

Annick Press Ltd.

THE CANADA COUNCIL | LE CONSEIL DES ARTS
FOR THE ARTS | DU CANADA
SINCE 1957 | DEPUIS 1957

We acknowledge the support of the Canada
Council for the Arts for our publishing program.
We also thank the Ontario Arts Council.

The editor wishes to thank John Ip, dancer, poet
and mathematician, for his valuable assistance.

Cataloguing in Publication Data

Baker, Barrie
   The village of a hundred smiles and other stories

ISBN 1-55037-522-9 (bound)   ISBN 1-55037-535-0 (pbk.)

I. Jorisch, Stéphane. II. Title.

PS8553.A3698V54 1998   jC813'.54   C97-932746-6
PZ7.B34Vi 1998

The art in this book was rendered in
watercolour, gouache, and pen-and-ink.
The text was typeset in Spectrum.

Distributed in Canada by:
Firefly Books Ltd.
3680 Victoria Park Avenue
Willowdale, ON
M2H 3K1

Published in the U.S.A. by Annick Press (U.S.) Ltd.

Distributed in the U.S.A. by:
Firefly Books (U.S.) Inc.
P.O. Box 1338
Ellicott Station
Buffalo, NY 14205

Printed and bound in Canada by:
Kromar Printing Ltd.

The Village of a Hundred Smiles

and other stories

The Trip

The Village of a Hundred Smiles was like a populous island in a sea of rolling fields. Everyone was happy with the isolated life. The soil produced all the food they needed, they traded for the few things they couldn't produce and news came to them by word of mouth. The people cheerfully

worked the land following the pattern
the Earth imposed on them in its year-
long journey around the sun. The rice
tax was always paid – somehow – and
there was always enough left to ensure
a fairly comfortable life for everyone.
The idea of willingly leaving the
Village of a Hundred Smiles was
almost unheard-of.

Grandfather received the message on a Tuesday after-noon in mid-spring. A dry-goods pedlar carried the note to Grandfather for two copper coins. The birds were singing in the trees, tiny shoots were popping up everywhere. The air was pleasant, warm and heavy with life. Spring-born piglets were squealing in the back yard sties, and there were ducks and chickens everywhere, pecking at seeds and insects. The world was fresh, green and delightful. How could it possibly be any better?

News of the letter spread quickly through the village. Everyone was excited; this was the first paper message anyone had received in more than three years. The last note had been bad news, so they felt a sense of forebod-ing at this new message from the outside world.

Grandfather understood how important this scrap of thrice-folded paper was to the entire village. He waited patiently in the yard until the people had assembled. With his right thumbnail Grandfather very deliberately eased the beeswax seal from the paper. Then he care-fully unfolded the tiny note and held it up to his face. His old eyes took a moment to focus on the elaborate characters. His lips moved silently as he worked out the meaning of the note.

"It is from my old teacher, dear friend and master. It was he who took me as his student and taught me to read and write. At his knee I learned of the wisdom of the old ones. At his side I journeyed over much of Asia. Finally, after four years, when the time came for me to choose whether I would return home or continue studying with him, he counselled me to return to the land and my own dear parents, who are now long departed.

"This same master now spends his scarce copper coins to invite me to the city to sit once more at his side, where we would discuss the meaning of our lives and other weighty matters."

9

"But Grandfather," called an incredulous neighbour, "you know that the city is many miles from our village. Why, it would take a young man at least four days to walk there, and with all respect, honourable Grandfather, it has been many years since you could be mistaken for a young man."

"What has the distance to do with anything?" Grandfather replied. "My old friend and former teacher has called for me. Of course I must go to him. The distance will melt as I think of the wonderful discussions and arguments we shall have. As for my age, of course I am old, but I have been saving my energy for just such an adventure. How could I turn it down?"

"Then you will go, Grandfather? You will journey to the city?" asked the neighbour.

Grandfather drew himself up straight; he did not like the tone of doubt he heard. He solemnly nodded his head. Many of the neighbours shook theirs.

"Well, Grandfather, if you are convinced then I'm sure we all wish you the best."

Grandfather remained firm. "Thank you; I shall leave in four weeks' time."

The crowd gradually drifted away and everyone went back to their tasks. Some people questioned whether a man of Grandfather's years could make such a journey. Others wondered why anyone with the great good fortune to be living in the Village of a Hundred Smiles would ever want to leave.

In the following weeks life went on as usual. People's activities were directed by the demands of field and pasture. Everyone was too busy to give Grandfather's approaching trip much thought. It was widely believed that he would wisely forget what he had said and stay at home where he was happy and safe.

Grandfather did not forget. He became more excited as the day came closer.

Then, one morning, when Grandfather arose he announced to his family, "Today I leave for the city to visit my old friend and master. Daughter-in-law, would you please prepare a package of rice cakes and vegetables that I could eat on the way?"

The family couldn't believe their ears. Grandfather was going ahead with this foolishness. It was a journey of many days. The weather was now very hot. The road was dry and dusty. Why would anyone, especially dearest Grandfather, want to leave the comfort of the village to trudge for days to a big strange city? Grandfather went on with his preparations as each family member tried to change his mind.

Finally he was ready to leave. He stood outside with a small bundle of food and a bottle of water.

"Well, I'll be on my way. Think of me often and fondly. I shall be thinking of you." Grandfather turned and gazed down the narrow, dusty road leading out of the village. It had been many years since he was chosen to study and left home as a young boy. Now, as he thought about the distance and his age, he realized that he didn't want to leave his family.

Granddaughter Little Orchid saw the slight change in his face and knew he did not want to go. She would have to think of something to help him.

"Grandfather, I shall certainly miss you while you are gone, and I will think fondly of you each day. But I wonder, dear Grandfather, if it is wise to wear your fine embroidered slippers on such a dusty road."

"Ah, you are quite right, dearest Little Orchid." He removed his slippers and handed them to Number One son, father of Little Orchid.

"Dearest Grandfather, your slippers are now safe, but what of your fine silk blouse, surely it too shall suffer from a long and dusty journey!"

"Once again you are correct, Little Orchid. I will leave my shirt with your patient father to keep safe until my return."

"Journey-taking Grandfather, your lovely trousers are much too rich to wear on a long and dangerous journey. Surely you will ruin them by walking in them through clouds of dust for days."

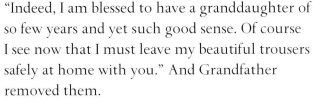

"Indeed, I am blessed to have a granddaughter of so few years and yet such good sense. Of course I see now that I must leave my beautiful trousers safely at home with you." And Grandfather removed them.

"Goodbye, family, goodbye, dear village! Wish me well," called Grandfather as he walked out onto the road carrying his bag of food and his water bottle, and wearing only his underwear. After a few steps Grandfather stopped; he noticed something was wrong. "Look!... No, do not look! I am out on the road in my underclothes! What am I thinking of? How could I make such a journey wearing only my underclothes? What would my friend and master say if I showed up at his door dressed as a baby or a beggar? There is nothing for it but to remain at home until I can solve the problem of clothes to travel in." Grandfather hurried back to the house, snatched his clothes from Number One son and quickly put them on.

"Grandfather, surely this is a sign that you are to remain with your loving family in your own little Village of a Hundred Smiles." Little Orchid spoke in a sincere and concerned voice.

The family sighed collectively as they realized that Grandfather would stay home at least until he had solved the clothing problem. But then what?

They did not have long to wait. Within three hours Grandfather was using his brush and ink to write a message to his old master on the back of the paper he had received.

This is what he wrote:

My dear friend and teacher,

I am unable to travel just now due to family responsibilities. Perhaps you would honour me and my family with a visit?

Your humble friend and student.

The message was given, with a bag of rice cakes and vegetables, to a pot-mender heading to the city.

Grandfather sipped his tea and watched the evening darkness gradually obliterate all signs of the road. He was very glad that he had changed his plans. He looked at Little Orchid. He was doubly pleased that his beloved granddaughter understood him so well.

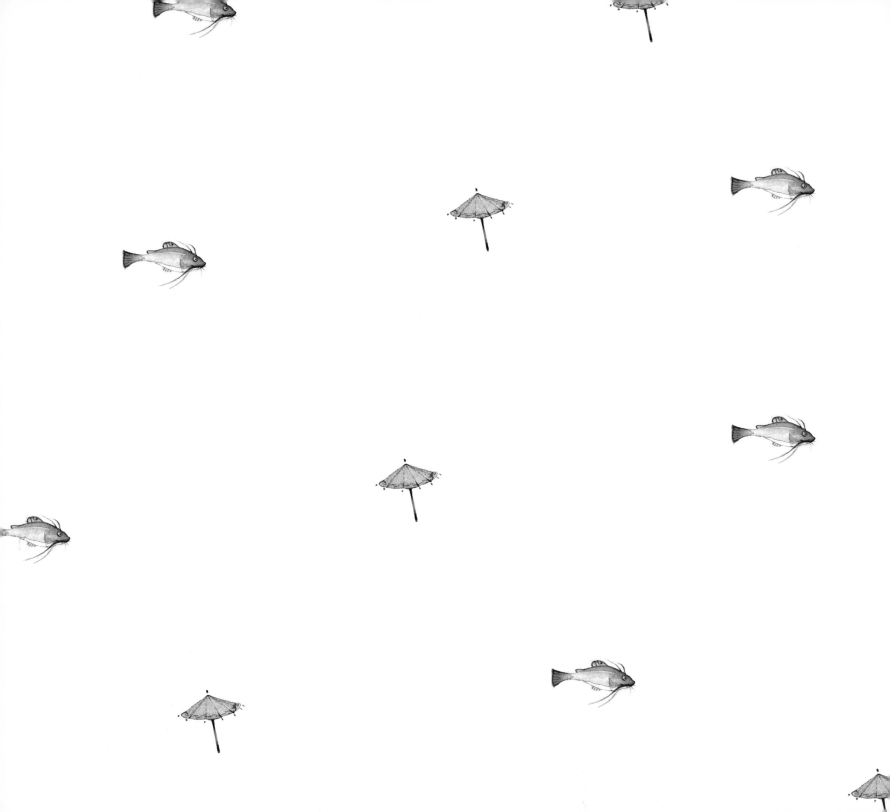

The Bicycle

The winter rain fell for the second week, and the main street of the Village of a Hundred Smiles was a sea of mud with large puddles in it. The family was snug indoors, telling stories and repairing broken tools and worn clothing. Grandfather talked about the old days when it really rained.

"I tell you the water fell so thick that fish could be picked out of it with your bare hands as they tried to swim upstream to the clouds. There was so much water the whole of the countryside looked like one enormous sea." His granddaughter, the beloved Little Orchid, listened to his every word, as usual.

"Oh, dearest storytelling Grandfather, is it true that the fish swam up the rain to the clouds, or are you telling your Little Orchid another fairy tale?"

"Well, you are right, I did exaggerate, but fish were found inland in pools after the water retreated. I myself took home two fine, fat carp, and my mother prepared them with peanuts and onions."

"Did you have a problem finding wood to cook your fish?" asked Number One son. "We are almost out of firewood and there isn't a stick of wood, wet or dry, to be found anywhere in the village." The family sat quietly after Father gave them his troubling news. Without wood they couldn't boil rice or noodles or fry vegetables or dry their clothes or take the chill off their little house. It would be bad to have no wood.

Meanwhile, upriver, Man-of-Thousand-Words — an honourable scholar, traveller and official messenger for some very important people — had a serious problem of his own. His bicycle was missing. It had been stolen, along with the tree to which he had tied it. Last night he had reached the Village of Wild Blossoms after walking all day in the mud. He was tired, hungry, wet and cold. He tied his bicycle tightly to a tree near the bridge and hurried into the nearby inn for tea, steamed noodles and a warm, dry rice-straw mat near the stove. While he slept, the river rose so high that its water reached the roots of the tree, and the tree toppled into the river, taking the bicycle with it. It did not take him long to figure out what had happened. Down the road he trudged, to the next village, to see if the tree might have come ashore.

The rain stopped in the morning, just as Mother was putting the last of the twigs under the rice pot. This would be the last hot rice unless they found some wood. They could start to burn the house, but they needed everything they had and there was nothing extra.

"Family, I will go out once more and search for wood – surely there will be some washed onto the land somewhere." And Number One son put on his jacket, took his rope and went out.

"Grandfather, what will we do? I cannot eat uncooked rice."

"Beloved Little Orchid, your mother is a woman worthy of praise in the kitchen; she will surely find us plenty to eat that does not require cooking. But I wonder how we shall make the tea that has such a calming effect at the end of the day. I will miss that indeed."

Number One son walked through the mud and splashed through the puddles, his eyes alert for anything to burn, but he had no luck; there was not so much as a twig. Then he saw it – an entire tree caught under their wonderful stone bridge. This was a large tree, a willow, and it would provide much firewood.

First, he must make certain that the tree would not drift away. He took his rope and made a loop around the largest branch he could reach. Then he looped the rope around a stone jutting out from the bridge and tied a sturdy knot. "I must get help," he thought. "There is enough wood here for three neighbours' families, but I must hurry before someone else finds my tree."

He hurried home, called three neighbours to come for firewood, got his axe and hurried back to the bridge. No one else was there. They would share the entire tree!

Grandfather and Little Orchid hurried along, trying to keep up to the band of firewood gatherers. They were all very excited at their good fortune. The men soon had many of the branches chopped off and were pulling the main trunk of the tree out of the muddy river and onto the shore.

"What is that ... that strange thing tied to our tree?" called one of the big boys. They all peered at the bicycle dangling from the trunk. When the trunk was far enough up on the bank that the current didn't suck at it so hard, they turned their attention to the metal object. Their choppers and knives made quick work of the rope holding the bicycle, and it was soon lying safely on the bank. As the rest of the group cut up the tree, Grandfather and Little Orchid examined the curious thing.

"Grandfather, what is this machine? It looks very strange indeed. I feel a little frightened by it. Look at those sharp, shining teeth on the little wheel!"

"I don't think we have to worry, beloved Granddaughter. It needs someone to do something to it before it becomes dangerous."

All of the wood was neatly chopped up and stored away in an hour or two. Then Number One son, as discoverer of the tree, took the bicycle in out of the rain. They all knew that metal will rust if left in the water, and this thing looked too precious to allow that to happen.

"The owner of this machine likes it very much," thought Number One son. "He had it tied tightly to a tree and it would still be safe if the bank hadn't washed away, causing the tree to fall into the river. Perhaps the owner will come looking for it. We will keep the thing clean and dry."

The sun shone, the village began to dry out, and the river returned to its banks and became more like its old self. Man-of-Thousand-Words searched the river bank for any sign of the tree that had stolen his bicycle. At last he reached the Village of a Hundred Smiles. In the noodle shop, over tea, he asked about a large willow tree in the river. Yes, he was told, a tree did get snarled up in the bridge. "Where is it now?" "Chopped up for firewood." "Who found it?" "Little Dragon, a farmer." "Where does he live?" "Is he in trouble?" "No, no, I would like to meet him." "He lives up the street, in the house with the butterfly painted on the door."

Man-of-Thousand-Words paid for his tea, took his leather bag and set out at a trot, looking for the house with the butterfly.

"Little Dragon, are you at home? Would you please come out? You may be able to help me."

Number One son knew what the stranger wanted. He had come to collect the beautiful, shiny machine with the wheels that turned around and the lovely little bell that rang when you pulled a lever with your finger. He didn't know what the thing was, but he wanted to keep it.

Slowly he came out of the house. "I am Little Dragon. I do not know you or what it is that you want."

"My name is Man-of-Thousand-Words, the scholar and carrier of messages for some important people. I believe you may have found my bicycle tied to the tree you chopped up for firewood."

"I do not know what a bicycle is, but I did find a strange metal object with horns that point backwards, two large wheels and a small wheel with teeth."

"Ah, truly that is my bicycle, my beautiful, shiny, black bicycle. If you tell me where it is I will collect it and be on my way."

"But how do I know that you are telling the truth? Anyone could come and claim this fine prize. Can you tell me more about it?"

"The horns are the handlebars, which I steer with, and on the right side there is a fine silver bell that rings when it is pulled with your thumb."

"The bell... You have convinced me that the wonderful contraption is yours." Number One son went back into the house and soon reappeared, carrying the bicycle over his shoulder. Man-of-Thousand-Words realized that people in this village had never seen a bicycle before. He had an idea.

He said, "For taking such fine care of my machine, I would like to give you and your family a ride."

"A ride? I don't understand." Number One son stared in astonishment as Man-of-Thousand-Words placed the bicycle on its wheels, stepped on the pedal and swung up onto the seat. The thing was moving! So was the stranger! They moved together: his legs went up and down and the wheel with teeth went around and the large wheels turned. Ah, but here was surely trouble – the bicycle was headed for a large puddle. What would happen now? – Amazing! The traveller moved the horn and the bicycle turned to miss the puddle. Then ... RING ... RING ... the bell called out louder than anyone in the family had been able to make it.

Little Orchid began to laugh in excitement. The whole family cheered; they had been listening and watching everything, and were now all out by the road to see the marvellous bicycle. They cheered as the visitor turned at the end of the street and sped toward them faster than a man can run. He stopped the bicycle and told Little Dragon to sit on the seat.

"You must sit absolutely still and hold onto the seat," he ordered. He steadied the wheel, put his left foot on the top pedal and pushed down. The machine surged forward and Little Dragon jerked backward. "Sit still and stop yelling in my ear." The traveller sounded more like the captain of a ship than the owner of a bicycle. Little Dragon settled down, and as the bicycle gained speed his face broke into a big smile; then he tossed his head back and laughed. He roared with the feeling of speed and freedom. His hair blew back. He heard the bell ring ...

Too soon, the traveller pedalled him back to his door. All the village was out watching, and when the bicycle stopped they all applauded. When he was back on the ground, Little Dragon spoke. "Master and Man-of-Thousand-Words, owner of the wonderful bicycle, would you allow some other member of my family to have the experience of flying like the wind on your marvellous machine?"

The visitor looked at the rest of the family – mother, son, granddaughter and grandfather. "Would any of you like a ride on my bicycle just like Little Dragon's?" The family shuffled their feet. Then Little Orchid stepped forward, only to be pulled back by her mother. "Mother, I would dearly love to ride on the bicycle, just as my honourable father did."

"Hush, Daughter, I don't think bicycles are for girls to ride on."

Grandfather stepped forward. "I would like a ride on your machine, and I would also like to ring the little silver bell as you do."

"Done," replied the visitor.

Little Orchid's sad eyes brightened. "Mother, would a ring of the bell the correct way be allowed?"

"Yes, Daughter, if our visitor agrees."

Little Orchid rang the bell while Grandfather balanced on the seat. She cheered as Grandfather moved away sitting up tall and stately. She laughed and jumped up and down as her beloved grandfather got off the bicycle at the end of his short ride and bowed slightly to all the neighbours. They clapped and bowed back.

Next, Brother rode, and then Man-of-Thousand-Words said farewell and pedalled out of town, ringing his bell.

That night, nearly every man and boy in town dreamed that one day he would own a bicycle. And Little Orchid dreamed that hers would have two bells, one on each side.

The Largest Kite

The winds of March began to blow, and all over the country people of all ages were building paper-and-bamboo kites. The daytime sky was never without at least one beautiful kite soaring, swooping or diving. In the Village of a Hundred Smiles, Grandfather was remembering the fine kites he made as a young man. He told of kites so beautiful that the brightest birds were put to shame, of kites so fierce-looking that brave men shuddered at the sight, of kites so large that they could lift a man high into the air.

"Oh, we knew how to make kites." And he smiled as in his mind he relived the tug of the kite string.

"Grandfather, dearest, beloved Grandfather," said Little Orchid, "how I wish I had been able to fly kites with you. We would have had such a wonderful time."

"Ah, yes, dear Granddaughter, indeed we would have enjoyed ourselves. It is unfortunate that we do not have our own kite now. Why, I would show you how to make it swoop and dive and climb and twist. We would have a wonderful time, if only we had a kite."

"Grandfather, is it so hard to make a fine kite, a little kite to fly with your beloved granddaughter?"

Grandfather sat very still and said nothing.

"Dearest, beloved Grandfather, could a girl of few years learn from her grandfather how to make and fly a kite?"

Grandfather sat quietly, and then said with growing excitement, "Fetch me the longest bamboo wands you can find. They must be dry, light and strong. There are some in the garden shed. Then bring me the beautiful paper that I have been saving, rolled up near my bed. Bring glue and string too, from the shed! We, my beloved Granddaughter, are about to build a kite. Not just any kite, oh no, but the brightest and biggest kite in the world!"

Little Orchid was always quick, but never so quick as when she gathered the material to make the kite. She nearly knocked her mother over as she ran into the house for the paper. She did bump into her father when she shot out from the shed.

"What is the rush? And where are you going with the fishing poles?"

"Excuse me, Father. Grandfather and I are making a kite. We won't break the poles." She rushed back to her grandfather.

Grandfather had cleared a large space on the packed dirt in the back yard, and he was just unfolding his pair of clever, sharp scissors that Little Orchid always wanted to borrow.

"Wonderful, wonderful. Now do exactly as I say. Lay the sticks out in this shape, and glue and tie them where they cross." Grandfather and Little Orchid tied, glued and cut paper all that day. The last line of glue was put on the last fold in the carefully fitted paper just as the last light in the March sky faded. Tomorrow, if the weather was right, they would test the kite.

When they woke up Grandfather told Little Orchid, "Go once more to the shed and get the very strong line that Father uses to fish for the big carp and sturgeon." By mid-morning the wind was strong enough for a test flight. On the ground, the kite looked much too large ever to fly. It also appeared too weak to stand up to the wind. Grandfather and granddaughter carefully carried the kite to a sloping, bare field, and he instruct-ed her to carry it to the top of the highest hill. She would then run down the hill, pulling the kite into the wind. As the kite started to fly she would give it more string, until Grandfather, who held the large ball of fishing line, would tell her to let go. Grandfather would then be flying the kite.

Little Orchid walked with determination up the hill, holding the kite above her; she looked like a beautiful little butterfly with black braids. She turned to face Grandfather and the wind. Then down the hill she ran, as quickly as she could. The kite pulled against the string in her hands. She gave it more string, the kite pulled, she gave it more. It is surely flying now, she thought. She wanted to look but didn't dare. Grandfather had warned her to keep running and not to stop until he told her to let go. Oh, why didn't he call, she wanted so badly to turn around!

Finally Grandfather called, "Now! Little Orchid, let go!" She released the string and turned, only to see their glorious kite climb steeply, then dive straight into the ground. At the last minute Grandfather gave the kite a little more line so it would slow down before it crashed. Little Orchid began to cry: all that work smashed to bits. Grandfather would be so disappointed. She ran to the kite, prepared to see it lying in pieces.

No, it was just fine! Just a bit dirty. What a fine, strong kite they had made. Grandfather was calling to her to pick up the kite and go back up the hill.

This time when she let go, the kite climbed quickly. Her heart seemed to go with the wonderfully coloured kite that held steady, high in the sky. Three swallows were diving at it, sure that it was some huge bird looking for dinner. The men and women working in the fields and paddies all stopped and looked up.

People working in their houses and shops stopped and looked out the windows or went outside at the cry, "Look at the kite of old Grandfather and his granddaughter Little Orchid." Then gradually all went back to work, leaving the two to their kite.

The wind started to blow harder. Grandfather said, "Ah, I had better tie the string around my body in case the kite pulls it out of my hands." So he tied the string around his waist. The wind blew harder, and Grandfather found himself pulled up the hill by his kite. At the top of the hill his feet left the ground and he was bouncing along, sometimes touching the earth, sometimes well above it.

Little Orchid was running after him, calling, "Dearest Grandfather, please stop playing and allow your little granddaughter a turn holding the kite."

"Granddaughter," puffed the old man, "I would gladly come back to you, but the kite seems to have other plans for me."

A stronger gust of wind caught the kite and took it and Grandfather both above the tallest trees. "Oh, dear, Grandfather shall be flown into the sun and cooked like a chicken wing in hot peanut oil. What a horrible thing for a loving granddaughter to see." Little Orchid put her hands in front of her eyes and peeked through her fingers.

"Oh, I am finished," murmured Grandfather. "I shall be flown into the sun and cooked like a chicken wing in hot peanut oil. What a horrible thing for an old man's favourite granddaughter to see."

"Grandfather, dear, beloved, so-small-in-the-sky Grandfather, I am frightened. Please come back to me!"

The same thought was in Grandfather's mind. He was so frightened that he could only gulp and blink as he sailed higher and higher. "Anytime now," he thought, "I shall begin to crackle." Of course he could never get to the sun by kite, but he didn't know that, and so he fretted as he jerked his arms and legs. He looked as if he were trying to swim.

After a few minutes the wind began to die, and the kite descended with Grandfather leading the way. Little Orchid was puffing from chasing the kite and her flying grandfather. She had been joined by three of the young men from the village. They grabbed him as soon as they could and quickly pulled him and the kite back to earth.

"Grandfather, why did you frighten me so? You didn't tell me that you were going for a ride with our beautiful kite."

"Dearest Granddaughter, your old grandfather promises not to take any more voyages of that sort. To be like a bird once is more than enough for me. Let us go home and have tea. We have some scraps of paper and wood left. I will show you how to make the smallest kite in the country."

And that is exactly what they did.

The Village of a Hundred Smiles

A rich merchant was being carried through the Village of a Hundred Smiles when he became very hungry. He thought, "I must have food soon, or I will be ill."

As his sedan chair moved through the street, his eyes searched the buildings until he spotted a noodle shop. "Ah, just what I need," he said. "Noodles steamed, fried, or in soup, but noodles it must be."

He ordered his bearers to stop walking and daintily stepped out onto the rice-straw mats his footman provided to keep his silk slippers spotless.

"Do you have fresh noodles?" demanded the merchant as he entered the steamy noodle shop.

"Oh, yes sir, very fine noodles," replied the noodle-maker. "What kind would you like? Steamed, fried, boiled, in soup? How, sir?"

"Well, let me think." The merchant couldn't make up his mind, so he said, "I'll have plenty of each."

"Yes, sir. While you are waiting, please have a nice cup of tea and some cookies." With that the noodle vendor began to prepare noodles. His wife, his two sons and his three daughters prepared noodles. His aunt prepared noodles.

The merchant waited patiently, sipping green tea from a china bowl and eating almond cookies. As he sat, he began to smell the fragrance of something he liked even better than noodles. Rice with bean curd and vegetables! He suddenly craved rice with bean curd and

vegetables more than anything. He clapped his hands. His servants gathered around him. He was soon back in his sedan chair and moving down the street, following the smell of rice, bean curd and vegetables.

The noodle-maker, his wife, two sons and three daughters all ran out onto the road, calling, "But what shall we do with all these noodles?"

"Do as you will. I'm sure you'll put them to good use," answered the merchant.

Around the corner was the rice shop of the Lily family. It was from here that the delicious smell of rice with bean curd and vegetables was coming. The merchant called, "Stop!"

He jumped from the sedan chair as his footman scrambled to put down the rice-straw mats to save his beautiful slippers.

"Quick, rice with bean curd and vegetables. Bring me plenty, I'm famished!"

"O rich and exalted one," began the surprised cook. "We have just cleared away the last of the rice and vegetables from our meal. Please, sit and drink some nice hot tea and have a few of these almond cookies. I promise you won't have long to wait."

The merchant sat on the rice-straw mats by the table and began to sip his steaming bowl of tea and nibble on a cookie.

Mr. Lily's wife, his four daughters, his aged mother and father, and his venerable grandmother, the second-oldest person in the village, set to work. They steamed rice, cleaned and chopped onions, cabbages, carrots, radishes and peppers. They fried the bean curd.

As their guest sat sipping his tea and nibbling more almond cookies, he began to smell something better than noodles, even better than rice with bean curd and vegetables. "What delicacy do I smell now? I believe it is carp with peaches and red sauce! That is truly my favourite!" He clapped his hands and all of his servants rushed up to

him. "Find me carp with peaches and red sauce!" he demanded. Within seconds his sedan chair was jogging down the street, following the aroma of carp, peaches and red sauce. Mr. Lily ran from his shop. "But sir, what about this great pot of rice and this wok of vegetables, to say nothing of the bean curd? What shall I do with it?" Down the winding street trotted the servants. A hand waved airily. "Do as you will. I'm sure you'll put them to good use!" came the reply. The chair bounced. The merchant bounced, but he did not complain. His mind was on carp with peaches and red sauce. He saw the shop with the fish sign outside.

The cook, his wife, his son, his daughter, his aunt and his wife's aunt began to prepare carp with peaches and red sauce.

Meanwhile, the hungry merchant drank more tea and ate more cookies. He began to feel less hungry. In fact, eight almond cookies and four bowls of tea had quite taken his appetite away. Just as the meal was about to be served, he clapped his hands.

"Make haste. We are late. We must be in the city by Tuesday, or I shall lose much business. Why are we wasting time in this shop?"

The servants hurried to put the small rice-straw mats down; then, with their master settled in, they picked up the chair and began to trot down the street.

"Stop!" he shouted, and before his footman could get the rice-straw mats, the merchant had splashed through the mud and ducked through the low doorway into the shop.

"Is that carp with peaches and red sauce I smell?"

"Yes, O honourable sir. May I offer you some? We can have it ready shortly if you wish."

"Oh, yes, yes, I must have carp with peaches and red sauce, that is my favourite dish in all the world. Carp, carp, carp, bring me lots and lots of carp!"

The distraught family called after them, "But sir, what about the lovely carp and the peaches and this red sauce?"

"Do as you will. I'm sure you will put them to good use."

The three shopkeepers were all standing in the street, watching as the sedan chair disappeared over the bridge and down the road. They all had the same problem: what to do with all the food? There was too much for their families to eat, and it was much too good for the geese and pigs.

They were silent for some time. Then the first one spoke: "That man made me so excited that I prepared enough noodles, fried, boiled and in soup, to feed at least thirty people. What shall I do with all of these fine noodles? They will spoil if they are not eaten soon."

The others nodded in agreement. "Yes, I know," said the fish cook. "We have cooked twelve fish and have added at least eighteen golden, juicy peaches, and the sauce, well, it's perfect. This is the best carp with peaches and red sauce ever cooked. Why, the Emperor himself would smack his lips if he were to try it. But it too will be ruined if it's not eaten, and eaten soon."

Mr. Lily looked very sad and sighed, "The best rice with bean curd and vegetables I have ever made is getting cold in my shop. What shall I do with it all?"

The youngest child had been listening to her father and his friends, and she had a suggestion. "Why don't we have a party for Grandfather? He is seventy-two years old this year. We could eat outside, right in that meadow." She pointed to a lovely field where the hay had been cut just one week earlier.

The three men looked at each other and then began to smile. "Go get the rest of the families. We will call the neighbours to the meadow for a celebration."

What a party they had!

Since it was a village, nearly everyone came and everyone brought some food of their own. They ate and drank and visited until well after the moon rose. When they finally got their children home and in bed, they had all agreed that they had had the best time of their lives.

BARRIE BAKER grew up on the prairies, in a house near a river bank. He and his friends found a playground in the prairie wilderness whose limits were determined only by imagination. Two of their favourite books were *Treasure Island* and *Robinson Crusoe*.

Today Barrie is a teacher who lives with his wife and a lot of dogs on Vancouver Island. One day he gave his students some basic characters to work into an exercise for a creative-writing class: a greedy, self-centred traveller and a group of trusting villagers. A year later his characters came back and called on him, inspiring the stories of this book.

Barrie tells aspiring young writers to write and write and write, to be critical of the work, but not judgmental about it.

Barrie and his wife are now grandparents, and he dedicates this book to grandparents and grandchildren around the world.

Born in Brussels, Belgium, **STÉPHANE JORISCH** grew up in a place that was called Lachine, meaning "China", since the French explorers were originally convinced that they had reached China when they landed in Québec.

Because his family lived on the St. Lawrence River, Stéphane spent most of his teens on the water, in anything that would float, propelled by motor, sail or oars. It was a great place to dream.

Stéphane's father was an illustrator of comic strips for European daily newspapers, and was a great influence on him. Only now does Stéphane draw faster than his dad. He believes that curiosity and a keen sense of observation are most important for an aspiring writer or artist.

Stéphane, his wife, their three children and three goldfish live in a house surrounded by other houses with many children in them. His aunts, uncles and cousins live very close by. So, in a sense, they all live in a Village of a Hundred Smiles of their own.